The Goose and the Golden Egg

What happens when you are greedy?

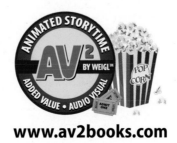

www.av2books.com

Go to **www.av2books.com**, and enter this book's unique code.

BOOK CODE

N 9 5 3 2 6 8

AV² by Weigl brings you media enhanced books that support active learning.

Published by AV² by Weigl
350 5ᵗʰ Avenue, 59ᵗʰ Floor New York, NY 10118

Copyright ©2014 AV² by Weigl
Copyright ©2009 by Kyowon Co., Ltd.
All rights reserved. No part of this publication may be reproduced, stored in a retrieval system, or transmitted in any form or by any means, electronic, mechanical, photocopying, recording, or otherwise, without the prior written permission of the publisher.

Library of Congress Cataloging-in-Publication Data
Fax 1-866-449-3445 For the attention of the Publishing Records department.

ISBN 978-1-62127-918-1 (Hardcover)
ISBN 978-1-48960-132-2 (Multi-user eBook)

Senior Editor: Heather Kissock
Project Coordinator: Alexis Roumanis
Art Director: Terry Paulhus

Printed in the United States in North Mankato, Minnesota
1 2 3 4 5 6 7 8 9 0   17 16 15 14 13

052013
WEP300513

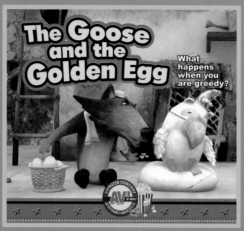

FABLE SYNOPSIS

For thousands of years, parents and teachers have used memorable stories called fables to teach simple moral lessons to children.

In the Aesop's Fables by AV² series, classic fables are given a lighthearted twist. These familiar tales are performed by a troupe of animal players whose endearing personalities bring the stories to life.

In *The Goose and the Golden Egg,* Aesop and his troupe teach their audience to appreciate what they have. Aesop learns that when he is greedy, he ends up with nothing.

This AV² media enhanced book comes alive with...

Animated Video
Watch a custom animated movie.

Try This!
Complete activities and hands-on experiments.

Key Words
Study vocabulary, and complete a matching word activity.

Quiz
Test your knowledge.

The Goose and the Golden Egg

What happens when you are greedy?

AV² Storytime Navigation

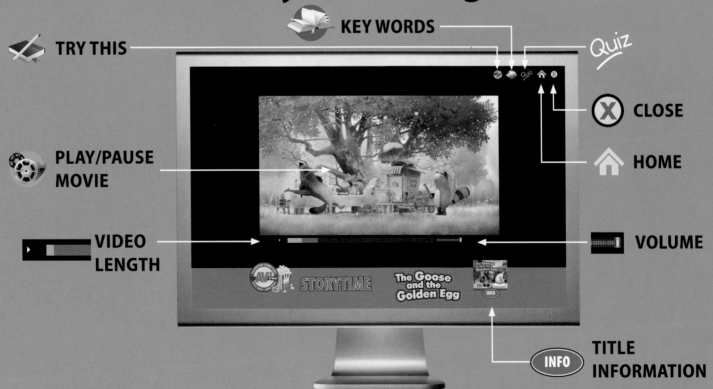

TRY THIS

KEY WORDS

Quiz

PLAY/PAUSE MOVIE

X CLOSE

HOME

VIDEO LENGTH

VOLUME

STORYTIME

The Goose and the Golden Egg

INFO

TITLE INFORMATION

3

The Players

Aesop
I am the leader of Aesop's Theater, a screenwriter, and an actor.
I can be hot-tempered, but I am also soft and warm-hearted.

Libbit
I am an actor and a prop man.
I think I should have been a lion, but I was born a rabbit.

Presy
I am the manager of Aesop's Theater.
I am also the narrator of the plays.

The Story

One morning, Aesop was fixing a wheel on the carriage.

Audrey and Milala were feeding the geese.

Goddard ran over and scared all the geese away.

Audrey and Milala were sad that they could no longer feed the geese.

"Why bother feeding geese?" said Goddard. "They are silly animals anyway."

The geese were close enough to hear Goddard. They thought he was being mean, so they chased him. Goddard ran away.

The geese gave Goddard a good scare. They thought it would teach him a lesson.

Presy was going through a box of old things.

She picked up a book and asked Aesop,

"What is this? I found it in the carriage."

Aesop was happy to see it.

"It's my notebook. I wrote a story in it when I was young."

Presy asked Aesop if she could read his story out loud.

"Sure!" said Aesop.

A long time ago, there lived
a poor farmer.
The farmer worked long and
hard to make money. He never
seemed to have enough.
One day, the farmer saw a strange light coming
from his goose's nest.
The farmer looked into the
nest and was surprised.
"It's a golden egg!" he said.

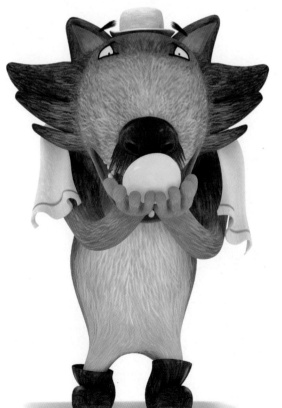

After that, his goose laid one golden egg every day.

But the farmer was not satisfied.

"I need more eggs to help my family. If I scare the goose,

I may be able to get all of the golden eggs out of it."

So the farmer crept over to the goose

and said, "Boo!"

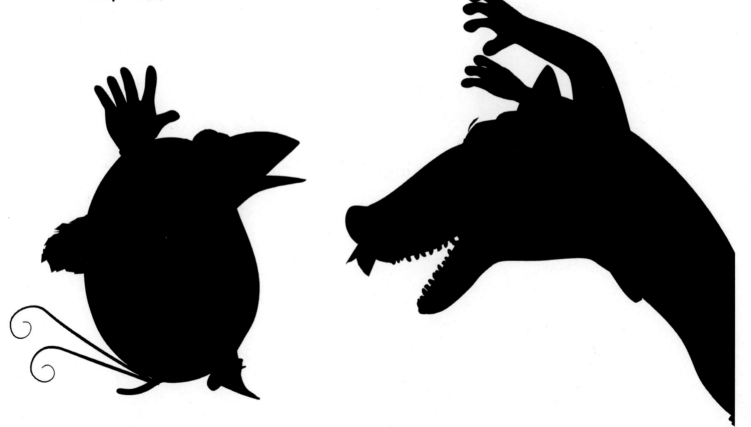

Presy stopped reading and showed
Aesop the next page.

"The story ended there," she said.

"Strange," said Aesop. "I thought I
had finished the story?"

Libbit was curious.

"What happens next?" he asked.

"Hmm, I can't remember," Aesop said.

17

Later that day, Audrey ran towards the group. She was holding what looked to be a golden egg.

Aesop, Libbit, and Presy were surprised.

"Audrey, where did you get this?" asked Aesop.

Audrey was holding a goose in her arms. "I found it under this goose," she said.

Aesop ran to the goose's nest and found another golden egg. "This is amazing! This is just like my story."

19

That night, Aesop was looking at the golden egg.

"I wonder how a goose made this?" said Aesop.

Then he remembered how the farmer had tried to scare the goose in his story. Maybe he would get more eggs if he did the same thing?

Aesop snuck up on the goose and her friends and roared.

The geese woke up and ran away from Aesop, honking in fear. They were all very scared.

Aesop found nothing in their nests. Only an old paint can. Aesop felt bad for what he had done.

The next morning, a raccoon wandered by. He noticed the golden egg on the table. "Aesop, why do you have a painted rock on your table?" he said. Aesop was confused. He explained that it was not a rock but a golden egg.

"I can smell the paint! There is no way that is a golden egg," said the raccoon.

Aesop sniffed the rock. It did smell like paint!

Aesop turned to the Shorties and asked them if they had painted the rock.

They all hung their heads in shame for lying to Aesop.

Aesop threw the rock into the bushes.

24

That same morning, Goddard was helping Presy clean out old boxes. Goddard handed Presy a page he had just found.

It was the last page of *The Goose and the Golden Egg*. Presy read the last page.

"Listen to the end of the story. The greedy farmer never got another egg after he scared the goose."

Aesop felt bad about scaring the geese. He went to find them and say he was sorry.

Aesop found the geese. They were hiding under the carriage.

"Come out geese. I learned my lesson about not being greedy.

What can I do to make it better?"

"You scared us so badly that none of us slept. We have

a long way to travel, and we are very tired," said the geese.

Aesop offered to let the geese ride on the carriage.

That way, they could rest while Aesop pulled the carriage.

The geese flew to the top of the carriage, and Aesop started to pull.

If you are greedy, you may end up with nothing.

What Is a Story?

Players

Who is the story about? The characters, or players, are the people, animals, or objects that perform the story. Characters have personality traits that contribute to the story. Readers understand how a character fits into the story by what the character says and does, what others say about the character, and how others treat the character.

Setting

Where and when do the events take place? The setting of a story helps readers visualize where and when the story is taking place. These details help to suggest the mood or atmosphere of the story. A setting is usually presented briefly, but it explains whether the story is taking place in the past, present, or future and in a large or small area.

Plot

What happens in the story? The plot is a story's plan of action. Most plots follow a pattern. They begin with an introduction and progress to the rising action of events. The events lead to a climax, which is the most exciting moment in the story. The resolution is the falling action of events. This section ties up loose ends so that readers are not left with unanswered questions. The story ends with a conclusion that brings the events to a close.

Point of View

Who is telling the story? The story is normally told from the point of view of the narrator, or storyteller. The narrator can be a main character or a less important character in the story. He or she can also be someone who is not in the story but is observing the action. This observer may be impartial or someone who knows the thoughts and feelings of the characters. A story can also be told from different points of view.

Dialogue

What type of conversation occurs in the story? Conversation, or dialogue, helps to show what is happening. It also gives information about the characters. The reader can discover what kinds of people they are by the words they say and how they say them. Writers use dialogue to make stories more interesting. In dialogue, writers imitate the way real people speak, so it is written differently than the rest of the story.

Theme

What is the story's underlying meaning? The theme of a story is the topic, idea, or position that the story presents. It is often a general statement about life. Sometimes, the theme is stated clearly. Other times, it is suggested through hints.

The Goose and the Golden Egg Quiz

1 Who thought that the geese were silly?

2 Who found the golden egg?

3 Why did Aesop scare the geese?

4 What happened when the farmer scared the goose?

5 How did the Shorties make the golden eggs?

6 What did the players learn?

Key Words

Research has shown that as much as 65 percent of all written material published in English is made up of 300 words. These 300 words cannot be taught using pictures or learned by sounding them out. They must be recognized by sight. This book contains 138 common sight words to help young readers improve their reading fluency and comprehension. This book also teaches young readers several important content words, such as proper nouns. These words are paired with pictures to aid in learning and improve understanding.

Page	Sight Words First Appearance
4	a, also, am, an, and, be, been, but, can, have, I, man, of, plays, should, the, think, was
5	always, animals, at, do, food, from, get, good, if, like, never, other, them, to, very, want, with
7	all, are, away, could, no, on, one, over, said, story, that, they, were, why
8	being, close, enough, he, hear, him, it, mean, so, thought, would
11	asked, book, found, his, in, is, it's, my, old, out, read, see, she, story, things, this, through, up, what, when, young
13	day, hard, into, light, lived, long, make, saw, seemed, there, time
15	after, every, family, help, may, more, need, not
16	had, next, page
18	another, did, group, her, just, later, under, where, you
21	for, how, made, night, only, same, their, then
22	by, heads, turned, way, your
25	about, end, find, got, last, say, went
26	come, let, started, us, we, while

Page	Content Words First Appearance
4	actor, leader, lion, manager, narrator, rabbit, screenwriter, theater
5	attention, dance, music, pig
7	carriage, geese, morning, wheel
8	lesson
11	box, notebook
13	egg, farmer, money, nest
18	arms
21	friends, paint can
22	bushes, raccoon, rock, table

Check out av2books.com for your animated storytime media enhanced book!

1 Go to av2books.com

2 Enter book code `N 9 5 3 2 6 8`

3 Fuel your imagination online!

www.av2books.com

AV² Storytime Navigation

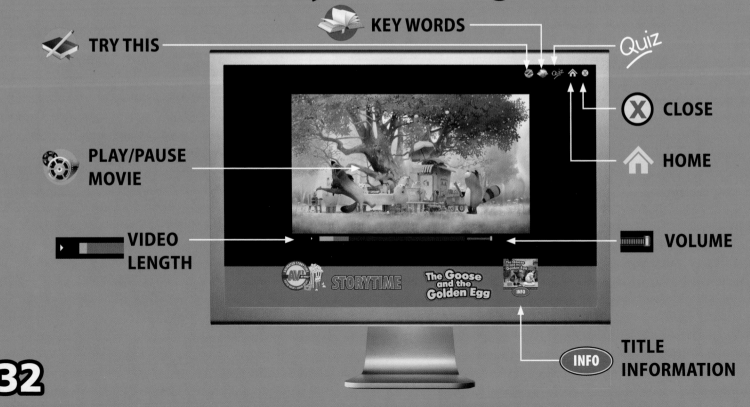

KEY WORDS

TRY THIS

Quiz

PLAY/PAUSE MOVIE

VIDEO LENGTH

CLOSE

HOME

VOLUME

TITLE INFORMATION

INFO